Bill: This book is about one of my favorite things to do: travelling to exciting new places, experiencing many new cultures, and meeting the wonderful people around the world! I have to say a big thank you to my favorite co-author (and son) Christian, who took over the reins for much of the book, as he helped research and write the majority of this book over his summer break. It was a labor of love for us to work on together, an experience we will never forget. Enjoy the book, and we hope it inspires you to go out and see the world!

Christian: This was a really fun book to write. With the opportunity to help younger kids understand travel and the many different places and cultures of the world, this turned out to be a perfect time to further share my passion of traveling. The process of writing the book was also exciting as I also learned more about the different countries and cultures around the world — the time and effort was really worth it!

oday was an exciting day for the Duck family! Lisa and Lance were leaving the nest for their first year of college. "Have fun and study hard," Lewis smiled. "You two are on a great adventure," he said.

That evening, Lewis received an unexpected call from his boss, Mr. Wood. "Good evening, Lewis! How are things at home?" Mr. Wood asked. "Oh things are great, Mr. Wood. Lois and I just dropped the kids off at college," Lewis responded. "You must be so proud, Lewis. I am calling to ask you to please come to my office first thing tomorrow morning," Mr. Wood said. Lewis wondered what Mr. Wood wanted.

What a surprise! That morning, Lewis walked in to see all his co-workers gathered in Mr. Wood's office. "Lewis, how do you like your new office?" Mr. Wood asked. "My office? But, sir, this is yours!" Lewis said. "Not anymore," said Mr. Wood. "I'm retiring and promoting you to President of Duck, Inc. Congratulations, Lewis!"

"It's time for you to really spread your wings and fly, Lewis," said Mr. Wood. "As you know, our company has offices all around the world. Your first big project will be to travel to all of them." Lewis knew it was time for his next big adventure!

Lewis rushed home after work to tell his wife the great news. "That's great, sweetie!" Lois said, hugging him. "Lois, since the kids are off at college, how would you like to come with me? It would be fun," Lewis said. "I would love to go! When do we leave?" she asked. "First thing tomorrow morning. We are going to New York City!" Lewis said.

The next day, Lewis and Lois took to the skies for New York City, landing at his favorite place to stay there, Homewood Suites by Hilton. "Welcome, Mr. and Mrs. Duck," smiled a friendly young man, handing over a key. "We've been expecting you. We hope you enjoy your stay." Lois and Lewis felt right at home.

Lewis spent the next few days visiting the office and sightseeing with Lois. They saw the Statue of Liberty, the Museum of Modern Art, Central Park, plus, they took in a Broadway play and had a nice dinner overlooking the city skyline.

S

oon they were off to see the world. First stop: Venezuela, where Lewis and Lois soared to Angel Falls, one of the largest waterfalls on earth. They explored deep jungles and forests, as well as interesting museums and shops.

N ext, they took flight over the ocean to South Africa and toured Cape Town, visited a world-famous botanical garden, and swam in the beautiful waters of one of the nearby beaches.

On their next stop, in Egypt, the Ducks saw the wondrous sights of the Pyramids and The Great Sphinx.

O

n they traveled, into Saudi Arabia. They visited the Kingdom Tower and also took a camel ride in the desert!

T he Ducks took to the skies once again and landed in Italy. They visited the Leaning Tower of Pisa, a building that leans due to a mistake made by the builders. Then they had a romantic boat ride in Venice!

Later that night back at their hotel, Lois said, "I'm having such a great time, Lewis. I've wanted to travel the world since I was a little duckling." "Well, there's a lot more left to see," grinned Lewis. They couldn't wait to continue their adventure!

Soon the ducks were in Paris, France, where they visited the Eiffel Tower, one of the world's most famous structures. They enjoyed eating in many of the wonderful sidewalk cafes.

In England, Lewis and Lois ate fish and chips; chips are what they call french fries in England, and they had tea in the afternoon. They toured Big Ben, London's famous clock tower, and the mysterious Stonehenge.

The Ducks soon arrived in Moscow, the capital of Russia. They trekked through the famous city streets of the Red Square and caught a special showing of the grand Russian Ballet.

In India, the lucky Ducks' first stop was the Taj Mahal, a magnificent white marble building built for an early Indian queen. It took over 20 years to build!

Next, they were on to China, which was Lois's favorite, as she loved the art and culture. She was a big help to Lewis, too, since she could speak Chinese. They visited the Great Wall of China, a very large wall built over 2,000 years ago to protect the country's borders.

Their next-to-last stay took them to Australia, known as "The Land Down Under." They toured the Sydney Opera House and visited the Outback, a desert area rich in wildlife!

Their last stop was Tokyo, Japan. Did you know that baseball is Japan's official sport? Lewis sure didn't. After the game, they waddled through a garden of blooming cherry blossoms. It was such a lovely sight!

A few days later, Lewis and Lois boarded the plane back home. They had such a great time, meeting many different people, seeing many different places, and learning a lot about the world around them. And Lewis couldn't wait to call the kids and fill them in on their around-the-world adventure!

The Story of Lewis

Our guests often ask, "Why the duck?
Who is he and what does a duck have to do with Homewood Suites?"

Homewood Suites chose a duck because it symbolizes versatility and adaptability. Ducks are comfortable in air, in water, and on land. They migrate long distances over extended periods. And their ability to adapt and thrive in a variety of places represents our goal in the travel and hospitality industry — to serve guests with resourcefulness and flexibility.

We chose a wood duck, considered one of the most beautiful creatures in nature. And we've given him a name — Lewis. By naming Lewis and bringing him to life, we've created a visual representation of a unique brand that caters to those who want the comforts of home when on the road for a few days or more. And, with Lewis to guide us, there is no doubt that we will meet our guests' individual needs for comfort, flexibility and convenience. Lewis also represents our desire to reach beyond our guests to the community around us through our Nature, Nurture, Learn principle.

HOMEWOOD SUITES
BY HILTON®

Author Bios:

This is Bill Duncan's fifth book in the Lewis the Duck series,
which includes *Lewis the Duck and His Long Trip, Lewis the Duck Goes to Canada,*
Lewis the Duck Goes to Mexico, and *Lewis the Duck Lends a Helping Hand.*
He lives in Memphis, Tennessee, with his wife, Julie.

Christian Duncan is no stranger to Lewis the Duck — this is
his third book in the series. He joined his father, Bill, in writing *Lewis the*
Duck Goes to Mexico and *Lewis the Duck Lends a Helping Hand.* Christian attends
Mississippi State University (go Dawgs!).

Artist Bio:

Greg Cravens is the creator of the syndicated cartoon, *The Buckets.* This is his
fifth venture with Lewis the Duck, as well. He enjoys spending time with his
wife, Paula, and sons, Gideon and Cory.